MICKEY VISITS THE DENTIST

by Ronnie Krauss
Illustrated by Disney Studios

The information on dental health contained in this book is considered by the American Dental Association to be in accord with current scientific knowledge.

Publishers · GROSSET & DUNLAP · New York
A FILMWAYS COMPANY

Library of Congress Catalog Card No. 79-55010
ISBN: 0-448-16582-1 (Trade)
ISBN: 0-448-13640-6 (Library)
Copyright © MCMLXXX Walt Disney Productions
World Wide Rights Reserved
Printed in the United States of America
Published simultaneously in Canada

"Gawrsh, oh gawrsh, I sure hope Dr. Choppers wins!" Goofy fretted, as he waited anxiously for the mailman to deliver the mail. "It would make him so happy!"

Back and forth, back and forth, Goofy paced. He kept his fingers crossed. A pocketful of good-luck charms jingled and jangled as he walked.

Goofy, Mickey and Minnie had entered the name of their dentist, Dr. Choppers, in the V.I.P. Contest of the Month run by the *Gazetteer*. (*V.I.P.* meant "Very Important Person.") If Dr. Choppers should be chosen as the winner, the Sunday edition of the newspaper would feature a story and picture of him right on the front page.

Every day Goofy had worn out a pair of shoes waiting for the mail, but so far no official-looking envelope had arrived. Today was the last day of the contest. If the mailman didn't have good news this morning, Goofy himself would have to break the bad news to Mickey and Minnie. How disappointed they would be!

When Goofy saw the mailman's cap bobbing up and down at the end of the block, he scrambled out of the house. "Could I please have my mail right now? I mean before it even reaches the mailbox? I'm waiting for a very important letter and . . ." Goofy looked at him pleadingly. "I just don't think I can stand it any more, not even for a minute!"

"Why, Goofy," the mailman smiled. "You must be waiting for something VERY special."

Goofy held his breath as letters for his neighbors filed by. "Let's see . . . Duck, B.B. Wolf, P. Pan . . . Goofy. Could this be it?" YES! IT WAS!

Goofy was so excited he could hardly open the envelope. He unfolded the letter. It said:

Dear Goofy, Minnie and Mickey,

Congratulations! By unanimous choice, the judges of the V. I. P. Contest of the Month have selected your dentist for this month's winner. If you will send us a photograph of Dr. Choppers by this Friday, we will put his picture on the front page of the Sunday Gazetteer along with his story.

Sincerely,
Editor, Gazetteer

"Whoopee! We won!" Goofy kicked his heels in the air. He read the letter again. Suddenly, his jaw dropped. "A photograph by FRIDAY?" he gasped. "But that's today! Omigawrsh, what'll I do?"

Then he had an idea. He would go to see Mickey. Mickey would know how to get a picture of Dr. Choppers without spoiling the surprise.

Meanwhile, Mickey was getting ready for his dental appointment. He brushed his teeth and looked at them with admiration. "Mirror, mirror, on the wall, whose pearly whites are the finest of all?" he asked.

A voice answered, "His teeth are brushed after food that's sticky, he flosses at night — his name is Mickey!"
Was Mickey startled! The mirror had answered him! He leaned forward and VERY CAREFULLY looked into

it again. But then he heard snickering behind the door. And there were his nephews, Morty and Ferdie, who knew Mickey's routine as he prepared to go to the dentist. They had planned the joke that morning.

They were still giggling when Mickey said, "I'm glad you're here, anyway, because I have a surprise. I made appointments for both of you to have your teeth cleaned. Then, afterwards, we'll go visit Minnie."

"Okay," the boys agreed, and they all set out for Dr. Choppers' office.

When Mickey and his nephews arrived, the dentist was busy with another patient. Mickey gave their names to the receptionist and sat down in the waiting room with Morty and Ferdie. He leafed through *Take Care of Me, Please*, *You Get Just One Chance* by I. M. Deteeth, and then he read part of *Sweet Tooth Gets a Toothache*.

The door opened and Dr. Choppers came out of the examining room. Minnie Mouse walked out with him.

"Hello, Mickey," she said. "Hi, Morty, Ferdie."

Minnie had just had her teeth checked and cleaned. "Look, Mickey," she smiled. "No cavities."

Her teeth looked so white and her smile was so dazzling, Mickey almost forgot why he was there. "You sure do a great job," he told Dr. Choppers.

"Well, *I* do some of it!" Minnie laughed. "Dr. Choppers was just telling me how important it is to eat the right foods, like fresh fruits and vegetables, instead of sweets. And I do! So," she added, looking at Morty and Ferdie, "I'll see you later for apples and oranges!"

Dr. Choppers motioned for Mickey to go into the examining room. "I'll be right there," he said.

Once inside, Mickey settled himself in the big dentist's chair. He put his head back on the padded rest and crossed his legs. Mickey found the dentist's chair very comfortable, and thought how nice it would be to have

one in his own living room. Then his thoughts turned to Goofy. "I wonder if Goofy has received anything from the *Gazetteer* announcing Dr. Choppers as V.I.P. of the Month," Mickey pondered. "I sure do hope he wins."

Now, as Mickey was wondering about Goofy, Goofy was also wondering about Mickey, because he had rushed over to Mickey's house and found that he wasn't home. "Gawrsh, what'll I do now?" Goofy thought. "I can't just go to Dr. Choppers and ask him for a picture—it would spoil the surprise. But I have to get a picture." Suddenly, an idea flashed in his head. "Ah-hah! I've got it!" he shouted. And off Goofy rushed.

Back at the dentist's office, Dr. Choppers entered his examining room to prepare his instruments. There was the metal pick called the *explorer*, which the doctor probed with when he was hunting for cavities. There was also a rounded, sharp-edged tool for cleaning teeth—the *scaler*. A glass jar full of cotton balls and a pair of special tweezers for picking up the cotton were on the table, too. Dr. Choppers was cleaning the little mirror-on-a-stick that helped him see into all the nooks and crannies of his patients' mouths.

When the dentist turned on the big overhead light that shone into Mickey's mouth, Mickey knew it was time to begin. Dr. Choppers fastened a bib around Mickey's neck and told Mickey to open his mouth wide.

"Beauties!" Dr. Choppers exclaimed as he peered in. "An all-star cast."

The dentist left the room and came back with a little piece of cardboard. "We'll take an X-ray picture to see what the insides of your teeth and gums look like, Mickey. Then we can be certain that there aren't any cavities beginning to develop."

Mickey bit the cardboard sandwich, and Dr. Choppers worked the machine. "There!" he said. "Now I'm ready to clean."

But just at that moment Mickey noticed a set of strange-looking teeth on top of the cabinet. His eyes nearly jumped out of his head. "What kind of teeth are THOSE?"

Dr. Choppers reached for the teeth, chuckling. "These are joke-shop teeth. A patient gave them to me for laughs. You wind them up and they chomp. See?" And Dr. Choppers proceeded to demonstrate.

"I'll bet Morty and Ferdie would get a kick out of those," said Mickey.

"I'm sure they would!" replied the dentist. Then, holding the teeth behind his back, Dr. Choppers opened the door and called, "Come in here, boys. I have something you might like to see."

Curious, Mickey's two little nephews entered the examining room. "I had a call this morning from the zoo," continued Dr. Choppers. "It seems a five-hundred-pound gorilla had a toothache, and they wanted me to pull his teeth."

"Well, did you?" asked Ferdie.

"Here they are," answered Dr. Choppers, and he whipped the joke-shop teeth out from behind his back and set them loose on the floor.

"Clackity-clack! Clackity-clack!" the teeth chattered noisily.

"YOW!" For a moment the boys were startled. Then Ferdie took a closer look. "Aw, they're not gorilla teeth. They're fake."

"Yeah," added Morty with a relieved chuckle. "We've seen some just like them in a joke-shop window."

"It's pretty hard to fool Morty and Ferdie," Mickey said, as they all laughed at Dr. Choppers' joke.

Morty took the teeth from Dr. Choppers, and turned them around and around, examining them closely. "Is this what my teeth look like inside my mouth?" he asked.

"Well, it actually is pretty close to what your permanent teeth look like when they have all grown in," Dr. Choppers said. "Here, let me show you." He pulled down a chart.

"When you are still a child, you have a first set of teeth, which are much smaller than the ones that will replace them," he explained. "As you grow up and your body gets bigger, you will need bigger teeth, too. So when you are about 5 or 6 years old, as you both remember, the first of your baby teeth falls out, and your permanent teeth begin to grow in. These permanent teeth will last the rest of your life, if you take good care of them. But you only get one set of permanent teeth. They could celebrate an 80th birthday if you eat the right foods, brush them after every meal or snack, learn to use dental floss once a day, and go the the dentist twice a year."

"Oh, we will," Morty and Ferdie promised. "We'll come to see you and do just what you say."

"Good," Dr. Choppers said. "So! As soon as I finish cleaning Mickey's teeth, I'll clean yours. And if you watch closely, you'll see exactly what I'm going to do."

BABY TEETH
CUSPID
INCISORS
MOLARS
PERMANENT TEETH
PREMOLARS
CANINE
INCISORS
MOLARS
WISDOM

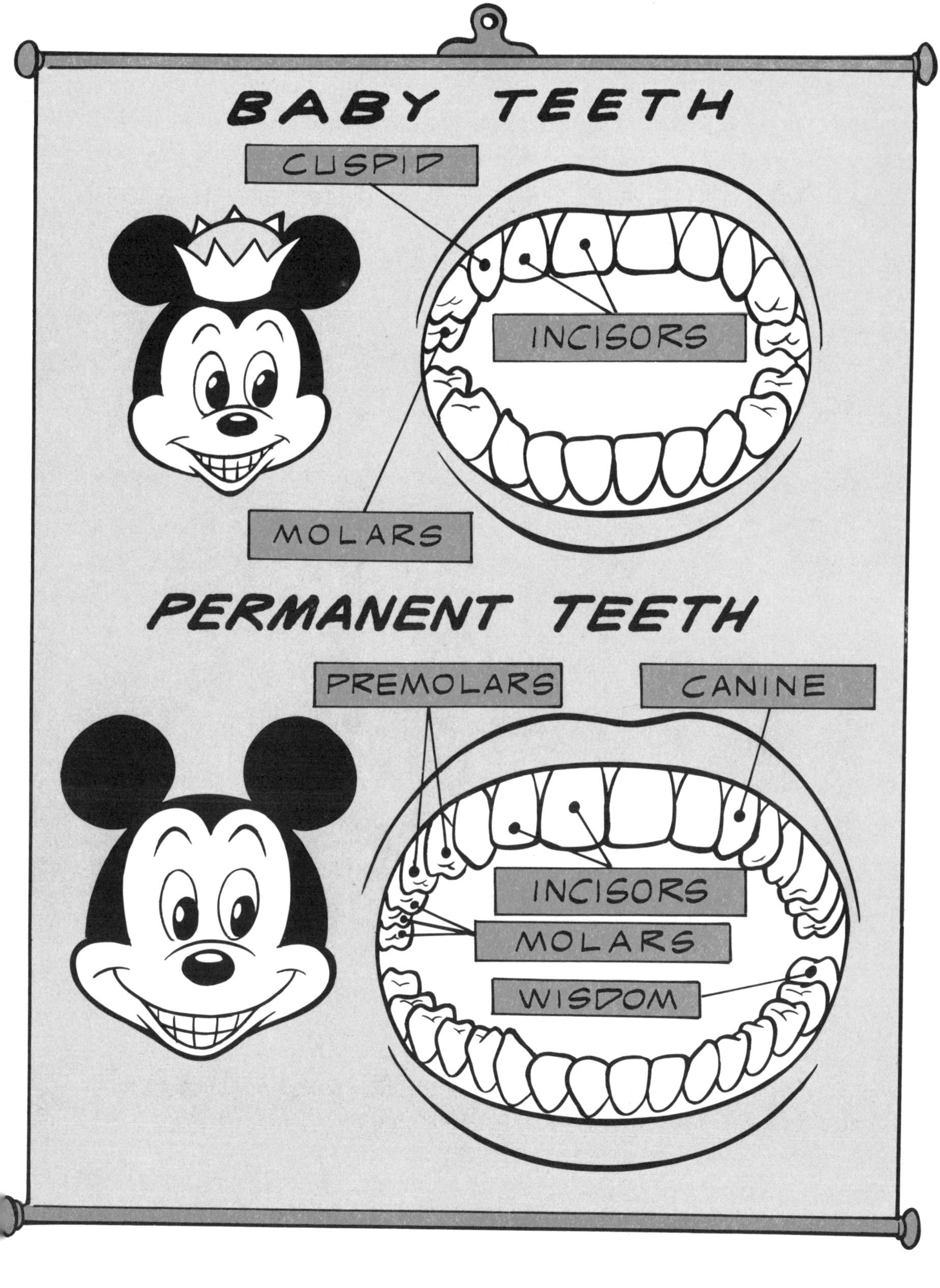

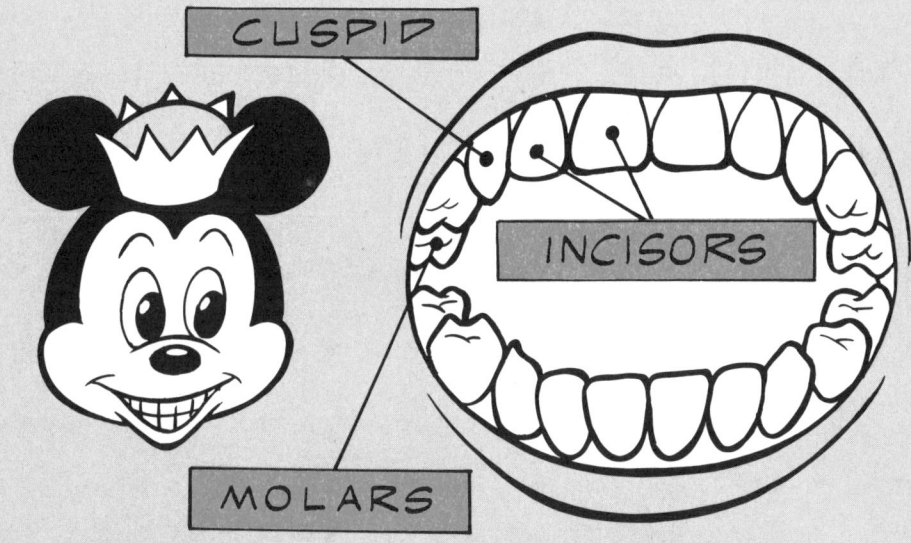

Dr. Choppers picked up the scraping tool. "I have to scrape the teeth to get them really clean," he explained. "If you keep your teeth clean, there's less chance of getting cavities, which are little holes in teeth caused by

bacteria. If I find a cavity when it is still small, it's easy to take care of, so the hole won't get bigger. I just clean out the decayed area with the drill and put a filling in the tooth. Then we know for sure that the decay has been stopped before it can cause any real damage."

Morty leaned close to Mickey. "Is the drill scary?"

"At first it is a little scary," Mickey admitted. "But then you realize that it doesn't hurt very much at all. It works quickly, and there is a stream of water and air shooting into your mouth at the same time, so it feels nice and cool inside. I always feel better just knowing that Dr. Choppers is taking away the bad part and preventing me from getting toothaches and infections."

Dr. Choppers attached a little rubber cup to his machine. He filled it with mint-flavored toothpaste and polished Mickey's teeth. Then it was Morty's turn. When he polished Ferdie's teeth, Ferdie giggled. "It tickles!"

Meanwhile, Minnie was glancing outside of her front window when she saw the strangest sight. "I'll be darned," she said to herself. "If I didn't know better, I'd think that was Goofy running down the street. But why on earth would he be dressed like that? I think I'd better find out!" Minnie dropped what she was doing and followed him.

What a silly picture Goofy made flying down the street wearing a trenchcoat so long it almost reached his sneakers! He had the collar turned up so it covered half his face, and the rest was hidden by a hat pulled down so

far it met the dark, goggle-style sunglasses on the end of his nose. A camera dangled from his neck, and Goofy clutched a clipboard. Pencils were stuck in all his pockets and behind his ears, too.

Minnie followed Goofy straight to Dr. Choppers' office, where she hid behind a tree and watched the most amazing sight she had ever seen.

At first, Goofy flattened himself against the building under Dr. Choppers' window. He seemed to be measuring something as he stretched his arms up. Then, after checking to make sure no one was watching him, Goofy slipped into the alley and returned with some garbage cans

and lids. VERY carefully and VERY quietly he stacked them until they almost reached Dr. Choppers' windowsill. Then up Goofy climbed—from can to can and lid to lid—until he was at the top. He held the camera over his head and pressed the button, and just after the FLASH

came a CRASH! as he lost his balance and fell. Down he came, with barrels and lids falling all around, making such an enormous clatter that Mickey and his nephews, who

were just leaving the dentist's office, came racing out to where Goofy lay stunned. And Dr. Choppers, who was still blinking from the flash, leaned out his window to see what was going on.

"Goofy!" Dr. Choppers exclaimed. "What are you doing here? And why are you in that get-up?"

"That's what I'd like to know, too!" Minnie said as she stepped out from behind the tree.

"Aw, gawrsh!" Goofy explained. "I thought if I came to Dr. Choppers' office disguised as a reporter, I could take a picture without spoiling the surprise."

Morty and Ferdie couldn't help giggling, Goofy was so funny. He just couldn't do anything right.

"Surprise? What surprise?" asked the bewildered Dr. Choppers, looking from Goofy to Minnie to Mickey. "What's going on here?" But Mickey and Minnie were just as puzzled.

Over the laughter of Morty and Ferdie, Goofy appealed to Mickey. "Remember that friend we entered in that contest? Well, he won, and they said they needed a picture, and I didn't have one..."

"Oh, now I see," laughed Mickey.
"Well, I don't," the dentist said, perplexed.

"It's like this, Dr. Choppers," explained Mickey. "Minnie and Goofy and I entered your name in the V.I.P. of the Month Contest, and you've won. Goofy was trying to get a picture without your knowing it so that you'd be surprised when you saw the announcement in the Sunday *Gazetteer*."

"Me? Very Important Person of the Month?" Dr. Choppers exclaimed. "Why, Mickey—Minnie—Goofy—I don't know what to say. What an honor! Thank you."

"We're the ones who want to thank you," Mickey said. "You always care about us and help us keep our teeth healthy. We think you deserve the Very Important Person award every month. And that's the truth!"

Goofy chuckled. "Don't you mean, 'That's the tooth'?" he said, and everybody laughed.

SUNDAY Gazetteer

DENTIST IS V.I.P. OF THE MONTH

DR. CHOPPERS, LOCAL DENTIST, IS A VERY IMPORTANT PERSON TO HIS PATIENTS

By unanimous deci of the citizens the area today wa awarded with the of approval upo shoulders of th kindly dentist offices which located in the ter of the sg